MARGRET & H. A. REY'S
Curious George
and the Dinosaur

Adapted from the Curious George film series
Edited by Margret Rey and Alan J. Shalleck

Houghton Mifflin Company   Boston

www.houghtonmifflinbooks.com

Library of Congress Cataloging-in-Publication Data

Curious George and the dinosaur/edited by Margret Rey and Alan J. Shalleck.
p.   cm.
"Adapted from the Curious George film series."
Summary: Curious George visits a museum with a class of schoolchildren and causes much
excitement by climbing up onto a dinosaur skeleton.
ISBN 0-395-51942-X
PA ISBN 0-395-51936-5
[1. Monkeys—Fiction. 2. Museums—Fiction. 3. Fossils—Fiction] I. Rey, Margret. II.
Shalleck, Alan J. III. Curious George and the dinosaur (Motion Picture)
PZ7.C918 1989   89-32366
[E]–dc20   CIP
                        AC

Printed in the United States of America

WOZ   30   29   28   27   26   25   24   23   22

Jimmy's class was taking a field trip to the museum,
and George was going along.

"We're glad to have you, George," said Mr. Chauncy,
the teacher, "but don't get into trouble."

At the museum, Mr. Chauncy began to explain
one of the displays. "These rocks are millions of years old..."
The students weren't listening.

"This is boring," said a student.
"It sure is," said another.
"When is lunch time?" asked a third.

George wandered off. He didn't find the rocks
very interesting, either.

But in the next room, George saw something very interesting.
It was a huge skeleton. What a long tail!

It was too much for George to resist.
He stepped over the rope and jumped onto the tail.

He climbed down...

…then he climbed up.

He climbed up and up until he reached the skeleton's head!

Just then, Mr. Chauncy and the class came into the room.

"Look at that dinosaur," said Jimmy.
"And look at George!" he shouted.
"Ride 'em, George," cried a girl.

The guards heard the noise.
"Get down from there," ordered one of them.
"I'm going to get the director," said the other.

George was scared.

"Is that how they rode dinosaurs in the old days?" a girl asked Mr. Chauncy.
"Well, no..." he said.
"Tell us more about the dinosaurs," someone said.

George was curious. What was a dinosaur?

"Well," said Mr. Chauncy, "the earth was once
full of huge creatures like this."

Suddenly, the director of the museum came charging in.
"What's this about a monkey on our dinosaur?" he asked.

"Guards! Get that monkey down before
he causes any damage," he ordered.

Poor George. There he was on top of a dinosaur...and no place to hide!

"Just a moment," said Mr. Chauncy. "George was a great help to me. He got the children interested in the dinosaurs."

"We wouldn't have listened," said a boy.
"It's so interesting," said another.
"I want to come back again," said a girl.

"Well," said the director, "I can see that our dinosaur isn't damaged. We'll forgive him this time."

"You can come down, George," he called.

When the bus stopped in front of George's house, the man in
the yellow hat was waiting. "I'm glad to see you, George,"
he said. "I hope you kept out of trouble today."

Mr. Chauncy said, "I have to thank you for making this visit an interesting one, George. But next time, promise not to ride the dinosaur."

"Hooray!" the students shouted.